Little Owl
Needs a Home

The Royal Society for the Prevention of Cruelty to Animals is the UK's largest animal charity. They rescue, look after and rehome hundreds of thousands of animals each year in England and Wales. They also offer advice on caring for all animals and campaign to change laws that will protect them. Their work relies on your support, and buying this book helps them save animals' lives.

www.rspca.org.uk

Little Owl
Needs a Home

By Sue Mongredien
Illustrated by Jon Davis

■SCHOLASTIC

First published in the UK in 2013 by Scholastic Children's Books
An imprint of Scholastic Ltd
Euston House, 24 Eversholt Street
London, NW1 1DB, UK
Registered office: Westfield Road, Southam, Warwickshire, CV47 0RA
SCHOLASTIC and associated logos are trademarks
and/or registered trademarks of Scholastic Inc.

Text copyright © RSPCA, 2013
Illustration copyright © RPSCA, 2013

ISBN 978 1407 13535 9

RSPCA name and logo are trademarks of RSPCA
used by Scholastic Ltd under license from RSPCA Trading Ltd.
Scholastic will donate a minimum amount to the RSPCA from
every book sold. Such amount shall be paid to RSPCA Trading
Limited which pays all its taxable profits to the RSPCA.
Registered in England and Wales Charity No. 219099
www.rspca.org.uk

A CIP catalogue record for this book is available
from the British Library.

Printed and bound by CPI Group (UK) Ltd, Croydon, CR0 4YY
Papers used by Scholastic Children's Books are made
from wood grown in sustainable forests.

9 10

www.scholastic.co.uk

1

Josh Fraser was feeling very excited.
Earlier that morning, the old stone barn
in Mr Walker's farm had been knocked
down by a wrecking ball. Josh hadn't seen
it himself, but there had been the most
enormous CRASH, so loud it had rattled
the windows in his classroom. Now
school had ended and, after a drink and
a snack at home, Mum said that Josh and
his best friend Tom were allowed to go
over there to explore the barn's remains.

"We can pretend it's a ruined castle
from the olden days," Josh said, putting on

his trainers in the hall. "We're the knights attacking the enemy."

"Yeah," said Tom enthusiastically. He and Josh had been learning about knights for their topic at school. "We'll invade the castle and seize all the treasures."

"Can I come, too?" asked Emma hopefully. She was Josh's little sister and six years old. "I'm good at looking for treasure. And Spotty Dog could be the knights' dog, sniffing things out." Emma was very keen on dogs and had about twenty cuddly ones at the end of her bed. Spotty Dog was her favourite — a blue and yellow toy with a patch over one eye.

Josh shook his head. "Sorry, Em," he said. "Only boys allowed."

Emma sat back on her heels, her hands up like little paws under her chin, and made a sad sort of whining noise.

Mum laughed at the sight. "Not today, missy," she said, reaching down to ruffle Emma's blonde curls. "You're a bit too young to go off adventuring with the boys. You can help me in the garden instead."

Josh laced up his trainers and turned to Tom. "Let's go," he said with a grin.

"I want you back here for tea, OK?" Mum said. "Six o'clock at the latest. And, remember, I'm trusting you both to be sensible at the barn. Mr Walker said it's fine for you two to go over there, and that there's nothing dangerous, but don't do anything silly, will you?"

"We won't," Josh promised. "See you later, Mum. Bye, Emma." Then they went out of the front door and headed down the road.

The farm was about ten minutes' walk from Josh's house and the two boys swished imaginary swords as they went, discussing which other weapons they might use in their knights game. Josh could almost feel his heavy armour clanking by the time they reached the farm.

"Whoa!" he cried when he saw the remains of the barn. The boys leaned over the wall and stared. Old red bricks lay scattered on the ground alongside some massive wooden beams that must have once held up the roof. The grass around the rubble was still speckled with brick dust.

"Cool," breathed Tom. "It must have been epic when the wrecking ball smashed it down. I wish we could have seen it."

"Let's pretend *we* did it with one of those massive catapult things," Josh said eagerly. "What are they called again?"

"Trebuchets," Tom said. They went through the farm gate and slowed as they approached the ruined building. "And a massive battering ram to bash through the doors," he added. "SMASH!"

"Come on, then," said Josh, grabbing a stick and holding it out in front of him like a sword. "CHARGE!" he yelled and ran towards the ruins, pretending he was fighting off the enemy.

Swish, swish. He dodged to the left
when an axe-wielding knight made a
swing for him.

Jab, thrust. He darted to the right to
avoid a missile from a catapult.

Beside him, Tom was doing the same.
"Take THAT, Lord Edward!" he shouted,
leaping over a pile of old bricks.

"We claim this castle as OURS!" Josh
cried, whirling his stick-sword around his
head.

"Hand over your gold this MINUTE,"
Tom ordered with a bloodthirsty roar. "Or
ELSE!"

The boys played for some time, chasing
imaginary foes and taking prisoners
mercilessly. Finally, all the enemies had
been defeated and the ruined castle was
won. The boys threw themselves down
on to the grass, panting after such an

energetic battle. "That was awesome," said Tom, sighing happily and rolling on to his back. "We showed them who's boss."

"Yeah," Josh agreed, gazing up at the clouds above. "And —" He broke off as a strange sound reached his ears. "Hey, did you hear that?" he asked in a hushed voice.

Tom propped himself up on his elbow. "Not Sir Harold, come to —?" he began, but Josh was shaking his head.

"No," he said. "I can hear a weird noise. Like an animal or something."

The boys both sat up and listened. Josh was right — there was a faint squeaking coming from nearby. "Is it a mouse?" Tom wondered, getting to his feet and gazing around. "You get loads of mice on farms, don't you?"

Josh looked, too, but he couldn't see

any signs of a mouse or another animal. He got to his feet and tried to follow the sound. "It's coming from over here, I think," he whispered, tiptoeing forward.

Then his eyes widened as he saw something moving in the grass nearby. "There," he hissed, pointing. "Did you see it? Look!"

The boys crept nearer, not wanting to disturb whatever creature Josh had glimpsed. "Oh, wow," Josh breathed when they were close enough to see. "Four baby birds!"

"They're so tiny," Tom marvelled, crouching down to look at them. The birds looked like four teeny balls of white fluff. Their eyes were tightly closed but every now and then, one would open its beak and make a little squeak.

"I've never seen birds so small," Josh said, talking quietly so as not to scare them. "They must have been living in the barn. Maybe they had a nest up in the roof or something."

Tom nodded. "Yes, and when the wrecking ball smashed through the roof, I bet these guys just dropped to the ground. Poor things." He looked a bit upset.

"They're lucky to have survived at all," Josh said with a shiver.

"We could easily have trodden on them," said Tom. "What do you think we should do now?"

"We'd better not go too close," Josh said. "Mum says you should never touch baby birds or eggs. The mother bird might stay away if there are people near her chicks."

"They must be hungry," Tom said. "And scared. Do you think they've been here all day?"

"I reckon so," Josh replied. "Let's go back and tell my mum. She'll know what to do." Josh's mum was a teacher and knew all sorts of interesting things. "Don't worry, we'll be back soon," he told the baby birds as he got to his feet. They stepped carefully away from the birds, then ran into the lane. "Come on, Tom, let's run. Sir Joshua and Sir Tom to the rescue!"

 2

Josh and Tom raced all the way to Josh's house and burst in through the back door.

"Home already? That was quick!" Mum said as they charged in. Then a worried look appeared on her face. "What's happened? Are you all right?"

"We're fine," Josh said, the words tumbling out in a rush. "We've found some baby birds up at the farm."

"They were just lying on the ground," Tom put in.

"We didn't know what to do—"

Mum put up her hands as the boys

talked over each other. "One at a time!" she said. "OK, let me think. I'm not sure what you're meant to do with baby birds. We'd better phone the RSPCA for some advice."

Josh knew that the RSPCA was a charity that cared for and sometimes rescued animals that were hurt or in trouble. They'd never had to phone them before, though.

"We got our dog from the RSPCA centre," Tom said as he and Josh followed Josh's mum into the living room where the phone was kept. Then he frowned. "Wait – I thought they just looked after pets, though?"

"No, they help creatures that live in the wild and farm animals as well as pets," Mum replied, leafing through the telephone directory. "Ah – here we are, there's a helpline number. Let's see what they say."

Josh and Tom perched on the sofa while Mum dialled and spoke to someone from the RSPCA. Josh couldn't stop thinking about the teeny birds. They were so small, like little pinches of fluff, smaller

even than ping-pong balls! Down on the ground, they weren't safe from cats or bigger birds, or even people's feet. Thank goodness he and Tom hadn't trampled over them, playing their game.

"No, there was no sign of the parent birds, according to the boys," Mum said into the phone. Josh wondered what had happened to the chicks' mum and dad. Had they been frightened away by the noise of the collapsing barn? It must have been so scary for them, having their home destroyed. He hoped they'd been able to fly to safety.

"OK," his mum said, still on the phone. "Yes, that's fine — we can do that. No, we won't disturb them. Great, thank you, that's very helpful."

She hung up and turned back to the boys. "The lady who answered said that the birds' parents often come back to feed their chicks, so we should go back and watch the babies from a distance to see if they do."

"But what if they don't?" Josh asked.

"If there's no sign of them after an hour or so, the lady said to phone the RSPCA helpline again and they'll send out one of their inspectors to take a look," Mum replied. She glanced up at the kitchen clock. "I'll just grab us some bits and bobs of food. We can have a picnic tea while we're watching the chicks," she went on. "Oh, Emma, there you are. Put your wellies on, love, we've got an important job to do."

Emma had changed out of her school uniform into her purple hoodie and some jeans. "What is it?" she asked.

Josh told her what he and Tom had found and Emma's blue eyes went very big and round. "Spotty Dog, you can come with us," she said excitedly, picking him up at once. "He would LOVE to see baby birds."

Ten minutes later, Josh, Tom, Mum and Emma set off across the village again, Emma with Spotty Dog tucked under her arm. Josh realized he was crossing his fingers as they walked. He really hoped nothing had happened to the birds while they'd been gone.

Once they reached the farm, Josh and Tom carefully picked their way across the rubble to show Mum and Emma the baby birds. Emma had to hold Mum's hand because the ground was so uneven.

"There they are," Josh said, pointing ahead. "Can you see them?"

"Oh my goodness!" Mum exclaimed.

"They really are tiny, aren't they? Don't go any closer, Emma," she said, as Emma took a step forward. "The RSPCA lady said we should keep our distance."

"They're so CUTE! I wish I could stroke one," Emma said, crouching down and hugging her knees as she gazed wide-eyed at the chicks.

"No, you mustn't, I'm afraid, love," Mum said. "It's very important. If the mummy bird comes back and thinks anyone has touched them, she might be frightened and fly away again." She peered more closely at the birds. "I think they're baby owls, you know."

"Owls! Cool!" Josh said. Last summer his dad had taught him how to make a really good owl hoot by cupping his hands in a certain way around his mouth and blowing gently through his fingers.

He tried to do it now and made a soft *Hoo-hoo*!

"But where are their feathers?" Emma said, confused. "They look fluffy to me. I thought owls had feathers?"

"Do you remember the ducklings we saw in the stream last week?" Mum said. "They were fluffy, too, weren't they? It usually takes a few weeks for baby birds to grow their feathers."

"Don't go too close," Josh reminded Emma, seeing her stretch out her hand towards them. He could tell she wanted to stroke and pet the chicks as if they were cuddly toys.

Emma looked disappointed but nodded, her arm falling back by her side. "Did you hear that, Spotty Dog?" she asked him sternly. "Don't scare the babies. No woofing allowed."

They walked a good distance away from the baby birds; then Mum opened her rucksack and pulled out a travel rug. Josh helped her spread it out on a grassy patch, and everyone sat down. "While we're here we can make sure nothing else disturbs the baby owls, as well as keeping an eye out for their parents," Mum said. She produced a thermos flask and four tin mugs. "Who wants some apple and parsnip soup?"

Mum was what you might call an adventurous cook and loved to try out weird new recipes. Some were disastrous. She had once made a raisin and cauliflower cake that was so disgusting even the garden birds wouldn't touch the leftovers. As for the fish and beetroot curry . . . Josh never wanted to *smell* that again, let alone have to taste it. Luckily, most of Mum's inventions turned out to be quite nice, if rather unusual.

"Yes, please," Josh said.

"Yummy," Emma agreed.

"Um . . . no thanks," said Tom, whose parents always cooked him ordinary things to eat, like sausages and baked beans. Even though Tom had been Josh's best friend since they were at playgroup together, he still wasn't convinced by Mrs Fraser's recipes.

Mum poured out cups of soup, then handed around shiny red apples and home-made fruity flapjacks. Tom examined the flapjack for strange ingredients before biting into it thankfully. They all kept their eyes on the sky while they ate, hoping to see the parent owls returning. The wind had dropped and they could hear the babies chirping louder than ever.

"Should we give them a bit of
flapjack?" Emma suggested. "They sound
really hungry."

Mum shook her head. "Owls don't
eat flapjacks or the sorts of food that we
have," she replied. "Boys, do you know
what they like for lunch instead?"

"Worms?" Tom suggested.

"Mice," Josh added. "Beetles and bugs."

"Yuck," cried Emma, pulling a face.

"That's gross!"

Mum smiled. "I think I'd rather have soup and a flapjack too," she said, "but yes, owls do eat that sort of thing. For them, a nice fat worm would be a real treat!" Her smile faded a little as she gazed up at the sky. "Let's just hope that Mummy Owl swoops down with something tasty for them to eat soon, or else. . ." Her voice trailed away as if she didn't want to finish the sentence.

Josh felt his heart thump. He could guess what she'd been about to say. How long would the baby owls survive without food? He stared desperately at the sky. *Please come back*, he urged the parent owls. *Your babies need you!*

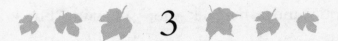

3

A while later, once they'd eaten and drunk everything, there was still no sign of any parent owls returning. The sun had sunk in the sky, streaking it with pink and orange, and now it was growing dusky and the temperature had dropped.

"Spotty Dog is getting cold," Emma said, leaning against Mum. "Can we go home now? I want to do some drawing."

Mum glanced at her watch. "We've been here over an hour," she said. "And you're right, Em, it *is* getting a bit nippy, and it'll be dark soon. Those little owls must be chilly, too, now that they no longer have the shelter of the barn."

"Why don't you phone the RSPCA again?" Josh suggested, pulling his jumper sleeves down so that they covered his hands. He couldn't help feeling worried about the baby owls. Why hadn't their parents come back?

"I will," Mum said. She rummaged in her bag for her mobile and dialled the number. "Hello, I phoned an hour or so ago about some baby birds my son found in an abandoned barn," she said once she had got through. "We think they might be owls that were nesting there. We were told to keep an eye on them for signs of their parents returning but I'm afraid we've seen nothing. I'm worried that they're getting cold and hungry."

Josh, Emma and Tom all listened hard

but they couldn't hear the other side of the conversation.

"I see, yes, we can do that. We live at Forge Cottage, at the end of Mill Lane. Half an hour, did you say? Yes, that's fine. We'll see you then."

Mum put her phone away and started packing up the picnic things. "We've got to carefully move the baby owls into a box and take them home to keep warm," she said. "Tom, your house is the closest. Let's see if your mum has got anything we can use."

"OK," Tom agreed. He, Josh and Emma folded up the picnic blanket together.

"I do hate leaving the chicks on their own," Mum said when they were ready to go, "but. . ."

"Spotty Dog will look after them," Emma said. She put her dog down on a

nearby brick so that he was facing the owls. "There."

"That's a very good idea, Emma," Mum said, winking at Josh and Tom. "Good old Spotty Dog. We'll only be a few minutes. Come on, then, let's head for Tom's. The sooner we go, the sooner we'll be back."

Tom lived quite near the farm so it didn't take long to walk to his house. "Hi, guys," said Tom's mum when she opened the door. "Do you want to come in for a drink?"

"Thanks, Lucy, but we're in a bit of a hurry," Mum said. "We were hoping you could help. Do you have some sort of box we could use, by any chance? And some gloves, too?"

Mum explained what they were doing, with Tom and Josh both adding other important parts of the story, like how they had stumbled upon the nest in the first place.

"Wow, well done for spotting them, boys," Lucy said. "Let me see what I can find."

Moments later, she came back holding a large shoebox and some gardening gloves. "Will these do?" she asked.

"Thanks," Mum replied. "That's great. And maybe a few tissues or some strips of kitchen roll, if you have any, just to help keep them warm on the way home. Thanks, Lucy."

It wasn't long before they were saying goodbye to Tom and his mum, and hurrying back down the lane towards the farm. Josh carried the box while Emma ran ahead. "We're back, Spotty Dog!" she called.

Josh caught up with her to make sure she didn't go too close to the owls. They were still chirping hungrily but he was convinced they sounded even weaker than before. He crouched down near them. "Don't worry, we're going to help you," he said, feeling sorry for the tiny birds.

Mum came and knelt down beside him. "If you hold the box, Josh, I'll lift them into it," she said. "Thanks, love. The lady on the phone said to wear gloves while I do this. I'll just put them on."

Josh and Emma kept very still and
quiet while Mum scooped up the baby
owls, one by one, and placed them gently
into the soft, tissue-filled box. They really
were helpless, Josh thought, watching
closely. Their legs were thinner than
matchsticks, their heads looked wobbly
and they didn't seem able to do anything
other than open and close their beaks in
the hope that food would be dropped

into them. They huddled together in the box, their eyes tight shut. It seemed a miracle that such tiny, weak creatures could ever turn into great swooping owls, able to fly and hunt.

"Shall I give them Spotty Dog to cuddle on the way home?" Emma whispered. "He could be like a duvet for the baby owls."

"That's very kind," Mum said, "but we don't want him to squash them by mistake. I think the tissues will be fine, thanks, poppet."

Josh felt a lump in his throat as Mum lifted the last bird into the box. This one seemed the smallest of the family, weaker and more fragile than the others. It swayed against the other three birds as if too wobbly even to support itself, and Josh exchanged an anxious glance with Mum. He desperately hoped that all four baby owls *would* grow up into big strong owls, but right now he just wasn't sure that was possible.

The RSPCA had advised Mum to keep the baby owls in a dark, quiet place once they were home, so Josh helped Mum take out a pile of soft towels and some sheets from a cupboard upstairs, so that there was room for the owls in there.

Three of the little birds were still chirping feebly but the smallest owl was silent now. Josh couldn't help worrying again as he peered in at them. "Do you think they'll be OK?" he asked Mum.

Mum hesitated before replying. "Let's hope so," she said at last, putting her arm around him. "Someone from the RSPCA should be here any minute. We can't do any more now, except wait and hope."

 **4**

"They're here!" cried Josh. He and
Emma had been watching through the
living-room window for the RSPCA
officer to arrive. It was much darker
now, and they saw the bright sweep
of headlights approaching before a
van pulled up with the RSPCA logo
painted on its side. Emma went back to
a game she had been playing with her
cuddly toys but Josh leaped off the sofa
and ran into the hall, almost colliding
with Mum.

Mum opened the front door and Josh

peered through the darkness to glimpse a
man dressed in a smart navy and white
uniform get out of the van. The man
went to the back of the van and took out
what looked like a toolbox; then he locked
the van and walked up the front path.

"Hello, I'm Bill," he said, holding out a hand for Mum to shake. He was very tall with broad shoulders and a big smile. "I'm an RSPCA inspector. I hear you have some unexpected guests with you this evening."

"We certainly do," Mum said. "Come on in and I'll show you them."

"I'm Josh," Josh said shyly. "Me and my friend Tom found the baby birds this afternoon. We heard them cheeping while we were playing. We think they might be owls."

"Good work," said Bill, shaking his hand, too. Bill's hand felt as big as a bear paw, warm and strong. "Well, I'm a member of the local owl group so I know a bit about owls. I can't wait to see your little fellas."

Mum led Bill up the stairs and Josh

followed behind. "It sounds as if you've done all the right things," Bill said. "Keeping them warm and away from danger is very important."

As they approached the cupboard and Mum opened the doors, anxiety took hold of Josh again. He couldn't hear a sound from the chicks any more. What if it was too late for Bill to help them?

"Here they are," Mum said, lifting the box out of the cupboard and showing Bill.

Bill peered in. "Ahh, yes," he said. "Well, you're right about them being owls. You've got four very young owlets here, only a few days old, I reckon."

"Owlets," repeated Josh. "Is that what you call baby owls?"

"That's right," Bill said. "I'm pretty sure these are little owls – that's a breed of owl. We have quite a number of them around here."

"Are they going to be all right?" Josh blurted out, gazing in at them, too. The four owlets were huddled in the tissues, very still and quiet.

"Let's see if we can get some food into them," Bill said, which didn't really answer Josh's question. "I've brought some with me."

"What, mice and worms and stuff?" Josh asked eagerly.

"Nothing so exciting," Bill said, smiling at Josh. "But some strips of raw meat that they should enjoy. Can we take the birds downstairs?" he asked Mum. "It'll be easier if I can do this at a table."

"Of course," said Mum. "They can eat at the kitchen table, like we do."

Josh followed Mum and Bill back

downstairs. Once in the kitchen, Bill opened his toolkit and put on a pair of rubber gloves. Then he took out a Tupperware pot and a pair of tweezers. "OK, chaps," he said, prising the lid off the pot. "Here's some dinner for you. You're going to like this."

Sitting at the table, Josh watched as Bill used the tweezers to pick up a single sliver of meat from the pot and gently hold it to one of the owlets' beaks. Immediately it opened its beak and began chirping hopefully.

Josh beamed. It was brilliant to hear them cheeping again. "They must be able to smell the meat," he said.

"Owls don't have a great sense of smell, funnily enough," Bill said, picking up another scrap of meat and giving it to a different owlet. "It's surprising, when

you think what amazing hunters they are,
but they rely more on sight than scent.
What I'm doing here," he went on, "is
just holding the meat against the owlets'
beaks. See? That gives them the message
to open wide for the food."

Just as Bill was saying this, the second
owlet opened up its beak and gulped
down the meat. "They're so hungry,"

Josh exclaimed, as the meat vanished in a single swallow. "Please will you feed that really tiny one next?" he asked. "He doesn't seem as strong as the others."

"He – or she – is a bit on the small side, you're right," Bill said. He took another shred of meat and put it against the smallest owl's beak. *Snap!* went the beak as the owlet hungrily gobbled it down.

Josh smiled, feeling a wave of relief sweep over him. Thank goodness. He'd been so worried about that tiny owlet but it was eating just like the bigger ones.

Emma came into the kitchen just then with Spotty Dog tucked under her arm. "Are you feeding the baby owls?" she asked excitedly.

"Come and see," Josh said, beckoning her over.

Emma made her dog sniff around the box and the pot of food, then sat next to Josh and watched as Bill went on feeding the hungry chicks. "Can we *keep* them?" she asked hopefully.

Josh already knew the answer: that owls were wild birds and shouldn't be kept as pets. Still, he couldn't help hoping that they'd be allowed to look after the chicks for a little bit longer. Imagine his friends' faces when he told them he and his family had four baby owls in the cupboard!

Unfortunately, Bill was shaking his head. "I'm afraid not," he said. "You and Josh and your mum have done an excellent job of caring for the owlets so far, but they're going to need lots of looking after, around the clock, so it's best if we do it. I'll take them back with me to the RSPCA wildlife centre when I go."

"They'll be better off there, Em," Mum added when Emma's chin wobbled. That always happened just before she started to cry.

"We'll look after them really well," Bill assured her. "We've got a special cosy box called an incubator, which will make sure they're kept at the perfect temperature. And we'll feed them tiny bits of food every few hours."

"Whoa!" Josh said. "Every few hours?"

"Yep," Bill replied, picking up a new bit of meat with the tweezers and giving it to the fourth owlet. Gulp! Swallow! Gone. "They only have very small stomachs so they need feeding little and often. We'll weigh them regularly, too, to make sure they're putting on weight."

"Can we come and visit them?" Josh

asked. He already felt very fond of the owlets, he realized, especially the smallest one.

"I'm afraid we don't really allow visitors," Bill replied. "We try to keep the centre as quiet as possible, especially if we're looking after wild animals. You're welcome to phone us tomorrow and ask how the chicks are getting on, though."

The owlets had all finished eating now, and seemed to be dozing, snuggled up close together. It was a very sweet sight, Josh thought.

Bill packed away his equipment and took off his gloves. "Right," he said. "Well, I'd better be off, then. Thanks again for what you did. I think your sharp eyes and quick thinking might just have saved these owlets' lives, Josh. Well done."

"Thank you," Josh said, feeling his face

turn a bit hot with the praise. Wow. How
cool was that – hearing that he and Tom
might actually have saved four owls! He
leaned over the box, wishing Bill didn't
have to go just yet. It all seemed so
sudden. "Bye, little owls," he whispered.

Bill slid the shoebox into a special carrier, then took it out to the van, along with his box of equipment. "Bye, then," he called with a wave, then started up the engine.

The three of them stood in the doorway watching. Emma's shoulders sagged in disappointment. "I wanted to give them names," she said. "Owly, Fluffy, Hooty and . . . and. . ." She frowned, trying to think of another. "And Little."

"Those are brilliant names, Em," Mum said. "Maybe you could draw a picture of them with your felt tips. We can post it to Bill at the centre. He might even stick it up by their box."

Emma rushed off at once but Josh stayed where he was. He watched the van disappear down the lane, feeling sad that the owl adventure had come to an end.

"They're in good hands," Mum said gently, seeing his expression. "Bill and the team will look after them really well, I'm sure. Better than we could have done."

"I know, but. . ." Josh scuffed his foot along the ground. "I hope they'll be OK."

"Me too," said Mum, giving him a hug. "But remember, Bill said we could phone for an update tomorrow, didn't he? So we can keep up with their progress. We'll ring first thing, don't worry."

5

Before he went to bed that evening, Josh asked Mum if he could use the computer.

"Don't tell me you're going to start your homework early?" she asked, pretending to collapse in shock. She put a hand on his forehead as if checking his temperature. "Josh, are you sure you're feeling OK?"

Josh grinned. "I'm fine," he said. "I just wanted to find out some more about little owls."

"Good idea," Mum said, switching it on for him. "I'd like to know more about them, too."

"Can I look as well?" Emma asked, lifting her head from where she was lying on the floor, finishing her drawing. It seemed to be of a nest and four smiling owls waving their wings.

"Sure," Josh replied.

"And then it's bedtime," Mum reminded them as she pulled the curtains in the living room.

Josh opened the browser and searched for "little owl facts", then chose a website. A picture appeared of a small, plump owl with brown and white patterned feathers, yellow eyes and a short beak, with a few paragraphs of information beside it.

"So this is what a little owl looks like when it's grown up," Josh said, reading the caption underneath. "Look, Emma. When our owlets get bigger, they'll look more like this."

Mum leaned over to see. "What a
beautiful creature," she said, then read
some of the text aloud. "'Little owls
mostly hunt at dawn and dusk. They like
living in lowland farmland with hedges
and trees, and sometimes nest in holes
in walls or trees. They have even been
known to nest in rabbit burrows'!"

"No way!" marvelled Josh. "I thought
birds' nests were usually in high places."

"Most of them are," Mum agreed.

"I hope the rabbits don't mind," Emma said, sounding rather indignant.

"They'd get a surprise, wouldn't they?" said Mum with a laugh. She read on. "'Unlike other types of owl, little owls often hunt in daylight as well as during the night. They eat small mammals, birds, beetles and worms.'" She winked at Josh. "You and Tom were right. Well done."

Josh clicked on a link to play a video about little owls. "Awww!" he, Mum and Emma chorused as the screen showed two little owls bobbing their heads up and down in a very sweet way.

"They look like they're dancing!" cried Emma, bobbing her own head up and down, too.

"The little owl doesn't hoot quite like other owls," said a man's voice over the video. "They have at least eight recognizable sounds."

Then came a series of little owl noises: one which sounded like *Keew!* *Keew!*, another that went *Hooo-ooo!* and then a very fast yelping cry.

"I thought owls said *Too-whit-too-whoo!*?" Emma said, flapping her arms and pretending to fly around the room.

"Well, some do, like tawny owls," Mum replied. "But little owls have their own special sounds, it seems."

"Little owls are so cool," Josh said, watching another video with three of them sitting on a branch together, all bobbing their heads up and down. He couldn't help thinking about the owlets over at the RSPCA centre. He hoped they were all right. Would they grow up big and strong, like the owls on the website?

He was about to switch off the computer when he had an idea. "Mum, can I email Dad about the owlets?" he asked. "I promise I'll be quick."

Josh's dad worked as a wildlife photographer, which meant he travelled around the world, taking photos of all sorts of amazing creatures. Although he and Mum had split up, they were still friends, and Dad sent lots of postcards to Josh and Emma from exotic places.

"Great idea," Mum said. "I bet even Dad has never seen owlets as young as our ones, Josh."

"Don't forget to tell him their names," Emma said, going back to her drawing. OWL CLUBB, she wrote underneath in big shaky letters.

"Come on, love, it's time you were in bed," Mum said. "Say goodnight to Josh

and go and put your pyjamas on. I'll be up in two minutes to help brush your teeth."

"Night, Josh," Emma said. "Thank you for finding the owls." She giggled. "Do you think they've got their pyjamas on, too?"

Mum smiled. "Probably not," she

replied. "Off you go. Quick!"

"Night, Emma," Josh called as she galloped up the stairs. Then he began typing his email, pleased to have something so exciting to tell Dad.

The next day was Saturday and the first thing Josh thought about when he woke up that morning was the baby owls. Had they made it through the night?

He bounced out of bed and ran downstairs to find Mum making porridge in the kitchen. "Can we phone the RSPCA wildlife centre?" he asked.

"Good morning to you, too!" Mum replied, laughing. "And yes, of course we can phone the centre, although I'm not sure they'll be open yet. Maybe you could have some breakfast first. Emma, breakfast's ready!" she called up the stairs.

Josh, Mum and Emma lived in quite a small cottage at the end of a lane but were lucky enough to have a big garden. As Josh sat at the kitchen table to eat his breakfast, he could see sparrows, blue tits and greenfinches darting back and forth from the bird feeder Mum had hung from the cherry tree. There was a friendly robin

who often came and watched Mum when she was gardening, his beady black eyes on the lookout for tasty worms to eat, and there were sometimes starlings, too, who tended to boss the smaller birds around like playground bullies. Josh had never seen owls in the garden before but he was definitely going to keep an eye out for them from now on, he decided.

Once it was nine o'clock, Mum thought the local RSPCA centre might be open, so she passed the number to Josh and he dialled it carefully.

A friendly-sounding receptionist answered. "Can I help you?" he asked.

"Hello, can I speak to Bill, please?" Josh said in his most grown-up voice.

"Bill. . . Let me see. . . Yes, he's here, I'll put you through."

Josh waited a few moments and then

Bill's deep, rumbly voice came on the line. "Bill Kennedy speaking."

"Hello, it's Josh. From yesterday? We found the owls' nest. I was just ringing to see if the owlets are OK."

"Hello, mate," Bill said. "Yes, they're doing great. They all survived the night and have been tucking in to lots of meat. We just weighed them, actually, and they've put on a gram or two already."

"Wow, that's brilliant," Josh said, beaming and doing a thumbs-up to Mum.

"But they are very small," Bill went on. "In fact, they're the smallest chicks we've ever had at the centre. We've had a chat about what to do and we think their best chance of survival will be to find them a foster family."

"A foster family?" Josh said. He knew that sometimes children had to go and live in a foster home when there was nobody else to look after them. But how did that work for owls?

"Yes, we can do our best to look after them here, but owls would do a much better job, and they do belong in the wild, after all," Bill explained. "So we'll try and find four little owl families who already have babies, and then slip an owlet into each one. Hopefully the parents will take care of them, along with their own babies."

"Oh, right," said Josh, imagining how surprised he, Mum and Emma would be if an extra child suddenly appeared in their house, needing to be looked after. "Is there anything I can do to help?" he asked.

"Actually," said Bill, "a bit of help would be great. I know from being in the local owl group that there are some nesting boxes in Ferny Woods. That's quite near you, isn't it? Maybe next time you're there, you could look out for any little owl activity and report back."

"OK," said Josh eagerly, thrilled at the thought of doing something useful.

"Make a note of anywhere you see or hear a little owl, or if you spot any signs that indicate an owl has been there," Bill went on, "and then let me know the details. It might lead us to a new home for the chicks, which would be great. Does that sound all right?"

"Yes, definitely," Josh replied, feeling puffed up with importance. "I'll ask Mum if we can go there today. Bye, Bill. Thank you!" He put down the phone and grinned at Mum. "The owlets are doing really well," he said happily. "And Bill wants us to help find them new families. Can we?"

"Of course we can," Mum said. "Maybe we could... Where are you going, Josh?"

"To get some equipment," Josh called over his shoulder, racing towards his bedroom. "This is an important mission, Mum!"

6

Once Josh had gathered together a pair of binoculars, a torch and a notepad, he ran downstairs and put them all in a bag. Mum was sitting at the computer, paying some bills, and glanced round at him. "Looks like you've got an email back from Dad here," she told Josh. "Have you got time to read it?"

"Yes, please," Josh replied, leaving the bag on the table. He sat down next to her and clicked on the little envelope on-screen to open the message.

Dear Josh,

Well done for saving the owlets! I'm really proud of you. Have you heard how they're doing since they went to the RSPCA? I've never seen birds in the wild as young as that before — I wish I'd been there too. How exciting! Good for you!

If you're keen to find out more about the owls, I used to have a great bird-spotting book which might still be in the cottage — see if you can find it. Inside there's lots of useful information about identifying different birds and I bet there will be some facts about little owls. I'm sure you already know this but remember to be super-quiet if you go out bird-spotting, so as not to disturb the wildlife. Let me know how you get on!

I'm still in New Zealand, taking lots of photos of the amazing wildlife here.

According to a website I found, little owls aren't native to New Zealand but they've been living here for the last hundred years, so I'm going to keep my eyes peeled for a sighting!

Give my love to Emma and Mum, and keep me posted on those owlets.

Love Dad x

Josh smiled as he finished reading. "Dad says he's got a bird-spotting book," he told Mum. "He thinks it might still be here somewhere. Do you know where it is?"

"Hmm," Mum replied. "I seem to remember there being a whole box of his wildlife books up in the loft. I said I'd look after them for him while he's on his travels. Let me see if I can track it down."

While Mum began searching in the

loft, Josh went to find Emma. She was in her bedroom, getting dressed in a mixture of fancy-dress costumes. When Josh walked in, he saw that she was wearing a red superhero cape, a fireman's helmet and some cowboy trousers, and was now trying to fit a pair of furry doggy ears on top of the yellow helmet.

"We're going out for a walk," Josh said, trying not to laugh. His little sister was very funny sometimes. "Um . . . maybe you should put on some jeans and a jumper?"

Emma snatched up a fairy wand and pointed it at him indignantly. "But this is my *superhero* costume," she told him. "What if I need to rescue some more owls? Or a lost puppy? Or a badger with a hurt paw?"

Josh thought quickly. "Maybe you should just bring the wand along, then," he said. "That way you'll still be able to do magic while we're out."

Emma twirled the wand with her fingers for a moment while she thought about this suggestion, then nodded. "All right," she said.

"Found it!" called Mum just then,

emerging down the loft ladder with a cobweb in her hair. She came into Emma's room holding up a small fat book which had a magpie on the front cover. *British Birds – A Spotter's Guide*, Josh read. "It's a bit dusty," she said, wiping the cover with her hand and blowing dust off the sides. "But there are lots of good pictures inside. And there's a whole section on owls, too – I checked." She held it out to Josh. "All yours."

"Great," Josh said, taking it from her and leafing through immediately. "Thanks, Mum. Operation Owl Watch is about to begin!"

Once Emma had changed out of her superhero costume, the three of them put on their coats and wellies, then set off for the woods. It had been raining overnight so there were lots of puddles in the lane that Emma insisted on jumping in, but the sun was shining now and a light breeze ruffled the leaves on the trees. At the end of the lane, they went through a stile and entered Ferny Woods.

In the woods, it was cool and quiet, with dappled light falling through the trees. Josh looked hard in all directions, hoping to see a little owl.

"Where are you, little owls?" Emma shouted, waving her wand around.

"Shh! You'll scare them away," Josh told her. "This is important, Emma. We need new homes for Little, Owly, Thingy and Wotsit."

"Fluffy and Hooty," Emma replied a bit sulkily. "My favourite is Fluffy," she said then, cheering up almost immediately.

"Which is yours, Josh?"

"I liked the smallest one best," Josh said. "Is that Little?"

"Yes," Emma replied, then suddenly shot out her wand. "Look! A squirrel! Maybe he could look after the owlets?"

Josh groaned but couldn't help smiling at the thought.

"Let's keep looking," said Mum.

Further into the wood, Josh saw a small bird with a pinky-brown chest that his spotter's guide told him was a chaffinch. Then they heard a strange drumming sound.

"What's that?" Emma asked, staring around.

They all listened. TAP-TAP-TAP-TAP-TAP! It reminded Josh of when Mum had hammered in little nails around the headboard of Emma's bed, so that she could hang up fairy lights there. TAP–TAP–TAP–TAP–TAP!

Mum suddenly pointed up at a tree behind them. "Look!" she whispered. "Over there!"

Josh and Emma followed the direction of her finger to see a black-and-white bird with bright red feathers on the back of its head clinging to the tree trunk. As they watched, it tapped its long beak rapidly against the bark, making the drumming sound they'd heard. TAP–TAP–TAP–TAP–TAP!

Josh's eyes lit up. "A woodpecker!" he said excitedly and pulled out his binoculars to take a closer look. "Wow." He'd never seen one before. Wait till he told Dad!

"Why is it *doing* that?" Emma wanted to know.

"I think it's probably looking for insects

to eat in the bark," Mum replied. "Their beaks are so sharp, they can go right through the wood."

TAP-TAP-TAP-TAP-TAP! went the woodpecker again. "It's a great spotted woodpecker," Josh said, finding a matching picture in the spotter's guide. "Ah — that one must be a male because it's got red feathers on its head."

"Good detective work, Josh," Mum said. "And a very handsome chap he is, too. Shall we move on now? Eyes peeled for owls, remember."

As they went deeper into the wood, they caught a glimpse of a rabbit vanishing into the undergrowth and Josh spotted a couple of pretty jays flying up above. "Ooh, toadstools, look," Emma said, squatting to peer at some bright red ones with white spots growing at the base of a tree. "Just like fairy houses."

"Remember not to touch them," Mum said. "If they're poisonous, they could make you very poorly."

"I hope the owls don't eat them," Emma said, looking worried.

"They won't," Mum assured her. She stood still for a moment, listening to birdsong. "There are certainly plenty of other birds here," she said.

"But no owls yet," Josh said, biting his lip. Operation Owl Watch was turning out to be harder than he had expected.

"Not even a hoot," Emma agreed.

They went on walking for another hour or so. Josh enjoyed trying to identify some of the other birds' songs with the help of Dad's book, but they still hadn't seen a single owl, or even a nesting box. Josh couldn't help feeling a bit disappointed. He had so hoped that they could find something which would help Bill rehome the owl chicks.

"Let's keep looking," Mum said. "And listening, too. Even if we don't see an actual owl, we might hear one. Or we might spot a nest in a tree."

They carried on walking, all listening

hard to the chirps and whistles of the
woodland birds. *Pee-wit pee-wit pee-wit!*

Seeee-seee-seeee!

Chi-chip-chirichirichiri!

Then, all of a sudden, Josh heard it.
Keeew! It sounded just like the little owls
in the video he'd seen on the computer.

Could it really be an owl at last?

He froze on the spot and clutched at Mum's arm. "Did you hear that?" he whispered excitedly.

She nodded, her eyes bright. *Keeew*, the owl went again.

Emma let out a squeak. "I heard it too!" she hissed, pointing her wand up at the trees. "Where are you, owl?"

The three of them stood still and gazed up through the swaying branches of the trees, all hoping for a glimpse of the owl. A few minutes passed but they didn't hear it again, or see it.

Mum shook her head. "I think it must have gone," she said, "but never mind. We all heard it, so now we can let Bill know that there's still at least one little owl living in Ferny Woods."

Josh felt really pleased. That might

mean the first new home for one of the owlets! He couldn't wait to tell Bill the good news. Then his eye was caught by what looked like a wooden box attached to the sturdy branch of a tree a short distance away. "What's that?" he asked, pointing it out to Mum.

She peered up at it for a moment. "I think it's a nesting box," she replied. "But I'm not sure what kind of bird might nest there. Let's go and take a closer look."

The three of them went over to the tree to investigate. The box was long and low with a small opening at one end and a sloping roof. "Oh, *yuck*," said Emma suddenly, kicking her foot around to try to shake something off her boot. "I just trod on some rabbit poo."

Josh glanced down to make sure he

wasn't treading in anything horrible himself – then blinked. What was that on the ground? "I don't think that *is* rabbit poo," he said excitedly, dropping into a crouch. "Mum, look. I think these are owl pellets."

"Owl whats?" asked Emma.

"Owl pellets," Josh replied. "I read it in Dad's book while I was waiting for you to get ready. It's a bit gross," he warned, "but owls don't chew food up like we do, they just swallow it whole. So if they eat a mouse, they eat the whole thing, bones and all."

"Yuck!" cried Emma again, her mouth falling open in disgust.

"And because they can't digest the bones," Josh said, "they. . . Well, they kind of sick them up again."

"YUCK!"

"And that's called an owl pellet. That's what you just trod in."

Emma let out a shriek and kicked her welly boot right off her foot. "I trod in owl SICK!" she wailed.

Josh was beaming. "No, it's brilliant," he told her. "Em — thanks to you, we just found out something really fantastic."

She was still hopping on one welly, arms outstretched to keep her balance. "What?" she asked, grabbing hold of the nearest tree.

"If there are owl pellets down here on the ground . . . then the nesting box up there must be one used by an owl family," Josh cried. "This could be a new home for one of the owlets!"

7

Josh was so delighted by their discovery that he wanted to phone Bill and share the great news. Mum had no signal on her mobile so she couldn't call there and then, but she used the camera feature to take some photos of the nesting box. Josh made a note in his pad of exactly where they had found it, too.

Meanwhile, Emma had managed to clean her welly boot on some grass and put it back on. She even changed her mind about the owl pellets when Josh pointed out what he thought was a bone visible in one.

"It's still gross," she said, wrinkling her nose, "but it's kind of cool too."

Mum delved in her pocket and found a small plastic bag. "Tell you what," she said. "Why don't we take a few of the owl pellets home with us in this? When we get back, you can put some rubber gloves on and pick through them to see what else you can find."

Emma looked doubtful but Josh's eyes lit up at once. "Could we? That would be epic," he said excitedly. "Then we'll be able to see exactly what the owls have been eating."

"Talking of eating. . ." Mum said. "Let's bag these up and go back for lunch." She grinned and held up a hand for Josh to high-five. "Score one for Operation Owl Watch! Good work, Josh."

"Hello, Bill, this is Josh Fraser again. I'm the one who found the owlets?"

"Hello, Josh Fraser again," came Bill's rumbly voice. "How are you?"

"Good," said Josh. "Really good, actually!" They were back home now and he'd rushed straight to the phone to call the RSPCA centre again. He could hardly get the words out fast enough, he was so pleased. "Bill, we've found a nesting box in Ferny Woods," he blurted out in the next moment. "And there were owl pellets underneath it, so it must belong to an owl. And we heard hoots, too, that sounded just like little owl hoots in a video we watched!"

"Excellent!" cried Bill. "That's great

news. Well done, mate. I knew I could count on you to help. Those nesting boxes can be tricky to spot."

Josh glowed with pride as he explained the precise place they'd found the nesting box. "And Mum's taken some photos that she can email over to you," he finished.

"Perfect," Bill said. "You've thought of everything. I'll tell the rest of the owl group that we think there are owls nesting there, and we'll check it out. Thanks again, Josh. Great work!"

After hot dogs with fried onions and squeezy mustard for lunch, followed by slabs of home-made alien cake (normal sponge cake with a whole bottle of green food colouring added), it was time to investigate the owl pellets. Mum kitted out Josh and Emma with some toothpicks

and an old pair of washing-up gloves
each. Then she covered the table with a
thick layer of newspaper and tipped out
the owl pellets so that they could start.

Josh set to work on the nearest pellet
with two toothpicks, using them to pull
it gently apart. "Whoa!" he said as he
uncovered what appeared to be a tiny
mouse skull. "Looks like this owl had
mouse for breakfast!"

Emma dropped her toothpick at once and backed away, looking horrified. "Poor mouse!" she exclaimed. "I think I might go and play with my dogs instead." And she peeled off the washing-up gloves and dumped them on the table.

"Wash your hands first," Mum called, going out of the room after her.

Meanwhile, Josh found it fascinating to work through the pellets to see what they contained. He found a few feathers and some scraps of grey fur as well as several other small bones. It was like being a detective, he thought with a grin, inspecting the evidence and trying to work out exactly what had been eaten by each owl.

"Wow," said Mum, coming back into the kitchen a short while later and seeing the collection of assorted bits in front of him. "What a lot you've found."

"Owls are cool," Josh told her happily. "And they must be really good hunters. Look how many bones there are."

"I wouldn't want to be a mouse living near that nesting box, that's for sure," Mum said, leaning over to take a closer look.

"Can you take some photos of these, Mum?" Josh asked. "Then I can email them to Dad to show him."

Mum ruffled his hair. "Of course," she said, then laughed. "I bet nobody's *ever* sent him a photo of owl pellets before. But knowing your dad, he'll be absolutely delighted to see them!"

Josh didn't hear any more from Bill or the RSPCA about the owlets for the next few days, and it was hard to concentrate at school when his mind kept drifting back to them. Had Bill been able to find four nests for them by now? Had one of the owlets already been moved into the Ferny Woods nesting box that he'd found? He hoped the chicks would all be well looked after by their new families.

On Thursday, Mum picked up Josh as usual after school. Emma had Gymnastics Club, so while they waited for her, Mum and Josh went to the local supermarket to get some groceries. They were just walking to get a trolley when they heard a shout.

"Josh! Is that you?"

Josh looked round to see Bill coming out of the supermarket with a bag of shopping in his hand. It must have been Bill's day off because he was wearing jeans and a T-shirt rather than his smart RSPCA shirt and tie. "Bill!" he cried,

feeling pleased to see him again. Now he could find out what had happened with the owlets.

"Hello, mate, I thought that was you," Bill said. "How are things?"

"Great, thanks," Josh said, followed immediately by, "How are the owlets?"

"They're doing really well," Bill replied. "Much perkier than when you first found them. Their eyes are open now, and they're gaining weight beautifully. Hey, and thanks for telling us about the nesting box you found. I went along with the owl group to have a look and you were spot on – there *are* little owls living there."

Josh beamed. "Brilliant," he said.

"That's wonderful," Mum agreed. "So when are you planning to rehome the owlets? Will that be soon?"

"Very soon," Bill replied. "In fact, me and the others from the owl group are planning to put three owlets in with new foster families tomorrow. We're going to give the smallest owl just one more day with us to make sure he's strong enough, and then we'll take him to the Ferny Wood nesting box on Saturday afternoon."

Josh smiled. "The smallest one is my

favourite," he said. "I'm glad he's going to be in Ferny Woods, near us."

Bill looked thoughtful. "Actually . . . if you wanted to, you could come along to watch while we rehome him, Josh," he said. "After all, you *did* spot the nesting box, not to mention finding the chicks in the first place. If you'd like to, that is."

Josh could hardly breathe with excitement. Would he like to go along? He couldn't think of anything more amazing. "Yes *please*," he said enthusiastically. Wait until he told Dad he was going on a real-life RSPCA adventure!

"That's really kind of you, Bill," Mum said. "I think you've just made Josh's year!"

"It's my pleasure," Bill said. "If you could drop him off at the RSPCA centre at about one-thirty on Saturday, that would be great."

"No problem," said Mum. "Thanks, Bill. We'll see you then."

"Bye, Bill," Josh said, unable to stop smiling. "See you on Saturday. I can't wait!"

8

Josh could think of nothing else as they picked up Emma and went home. He couldn't believe that Little was going to be living so close to them. And he couldn't believe that Bill had asked if he'd like to go along and help rehome him. How cool was that?!

Josh wished he could speak to his dad about it, but it was difficult to phone him while he was in New Zealand because of the time difference between the two countries. It was four-thirty on Thursday afternoon now for Josh, Mum and Emma, which meant it was four-thirty on Friday morning the next day for Dad. He certainly wouldn't be very pleased to be woken up by a phone call, even if it *was* with very exciting owl news!

When they got home, Emma began practising her headstands in the middle of the living room in front of her "audience", a row of cuddly toys, while Josh helped Mum unpack the shopping in the kitchen.

"Can I go on the computer again, please?" Josh asked when they'd finished. "I want to email Dad to tell him what Bill's just said."

Mum smiled. "I thought you might," she said. "Yes, of course."

Mum switched on the computer for Josh and opened the email page of the browser. "Dad's sent me another message,"

Josh said, spotting a new envelope symbol
on the screen. He sat down to open it at
once.

Dear Josh,
Wow! Fantastic owl pellet photos!! I
remember finding some of those and doing
exactly the same when I was about your
age, although Grandma wasn't very pleased,

as I used a knife and fork to cut into the
pellets and got mess everywhere.

I'm off to a place called Codfish Island
tomorrow, hoping to spot a really rare bird:
the kakapo, also known as the owl parrot!
Have a look at the picture I'm attaching —
it's the heaviest parrot in the world, and
can't fly. There are also parakeets, penguins
and lots of other seabirds — should be
fun. Then in two weeks' time I'll be back
in the UK, seeing the best creatures in
the whole world: you and Emma! Really
looking forward to it.

Love Dad x

Josh was delighted to hear Dad would
be home soon and immediately wrote a
long email back telling him about seeing
Bill, and how he was going to join him
on Saturday to help on such an important

job. Dad, of all people, would understand just how excited he felt.

The best bit of all, he wrote, *is that I'll know where Little's nest is, so whenever we go for walks nearby afterwards, I can listen out for him hooting. Maybe I'll even see him flying about when he's older! If you want, I can show you the nesting box when you're home.*

Emma came over and Josh read her Dad's email. "Tell him I can do a *really* good cartwheel now," she said. "Even better than Lottie's. And tell him Miss Fields has put my painting of Spotty Dog on the classroom wall. Oh, and please can he email me a photo of the funny parrot if he sees one? They sound cool."

"Sure," said Josh, typing all of this in a PS at the end of his email. Then he pressed send.

Emma leaned her head against him.

"Thanks, Josh," she said. "I hope Little has a nice big brother like you in his new home. Do you think he will?"

"That would be good," said Josh, and smiled. "I'm looking forward to finding out."

"Here we are," said Mum, slowing down as they approached the large RSPCA building. It was Saturday now, and the morning had gone by so slowly. Even making chocolate brownies hadn't made the time pass any faster. At last, though, it was time for Josh to go owl rehoming. Hooray!

Josh peered out of the car window eagerly. It was amazing to think about all the hundreds and hundreds of animals whose lives had been saved inside that very building. Working for the RSPCA must be so cool, he decided.

Mum parked the car, and then they got out. Josh was all ready for action with his binoculars, spotter's guide and notepad packed in a rucksack. "Let's go," he said, heading for the main doors.

Inside, there was a reception desk with a small waiting area to one side, the walls covered with posters of wild animals. Mum, Josh and Emma went over to the desk. "We're here to meet Bill," Mum said at the counter. "This is Josh Fraser, my son, who's going to help with an owl rehoming."

The receptionist was a friendly-looking man with glasses and curly black hair. "Ahh, yes, Bill told me about this," he said, smiling at Josh. "Take a seat and I'll let him know you're here."

They sat down in the waiting area for a few minutes, until they heard a familiar voice. "Is that Josh? Hello again! Do you want to come and see our little owl?"

Josh jumped up with a grin. "Yes, please!"

"Can we see him, too?" Emma asked Bill hopefully.

"Of course you can. Come this way and you can see how big and strong he looks these days."

Josh, Mum and Emma followed Bill through the centre to a quiet room at the back. On a table inside was a bird carrier, and Josh went over at once to peer in. Gone was the tiny helpless chick . . . and inside was a plump young owl, still grey and fuzzy but at least double the size he had been when Josh and Tom had first found the abandoned owlets. He was

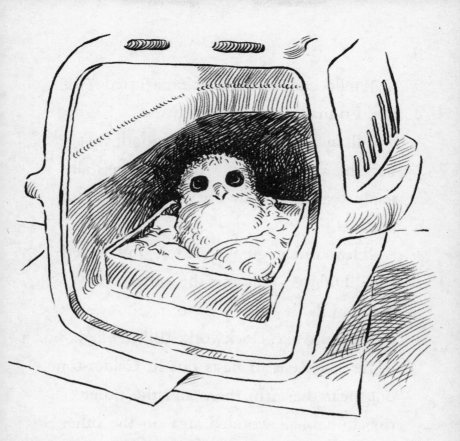

sitting in a small box filled with tissue
paper and he cheeped up at Josh, Emma
and Mum as they gazed in, his big yellow
eyes wide and alert.

"Wow, he's really grown!" Josh
exclaimed.

"He looks so much stronger," said Mum.

"Hello again, Little," Emma cried. "It's me, Emma!"

Bill smiled. "He's looking good, isn't he?" he said proudly. "And now he's all ready to go back to the wild, where he belongs."

"How did it go yesterday?" Josh asked Bill. "Did you rehome the other three owlets OK?"

"It went like clockwork," Bill replied. "They all went to nests out in Calderstone, one near the farm there and the other two in a small wooded area on the other side of the village. We'll go back in a few weeks to check up on them, at which point the owl group will ring them."

"They'll *ring* them?" Emma looked puzzled. "On the *phone*?"

"Not quite," Bill replied with a grin. Josh smiled, too, at the thought of the owlets holding a telephone receiver and chatting into it.

"Ringing birds is when you put a tiny band with a special identification number around one of their legs," Bill explained. "That way birds can be tracked around the country, and we can get useful information about them."

"Cool," said Josh. He glanced in again at Little, hardly able to imagine a band small enough to fit around his tiny legs.

"I suppose we'd better leave you to get on with the job, then," Mum said. "Hope it all goes well today."

"We made brownies for you," Emma remembered just then, holding up the bag. "Mum said it might be hungry work."

"She's absolutely right," Bill said gravely, accepting the bag. "In my opinion, any kind of job goes better if there are brownies involved." He smiled at Mum. "Thanks for these – and for bringing Josh. I'll give you a buzz when we're finished." He turned to Josh. "Ready, young man? I'll just find Jada, my colleague, then we'll head off."

Jada was a pretty Indian woman with long glossy black hair and a sparkly red nose stud. "Good to meet you, Josh," she said, shaking his hand. "Bill's told me all about your excellent owl rescue. Now for some excellent owl rehoming!"

"Definitely," Josh replied with a smile.

Bill took the bird carrier out to the car park, where a couple of RSPCA vans stood waiting for use. He unlocked the nearest one and opened the back door so that Josh could climb inside, then showed him where to clip in his seatbelt. After they'd put Little's bird carrier securely in the back of the van, Bill and Jada got into the front, then Bill started the engine and they set off.

"According to the owl group, the nesting box you found in Ferny Woods already has three chicks inside," Bill told him. "The chicks are slightly older than our little chap, but we're hoping that the parents will accept him."

"Fingers crossed," said Josh.

"Some of Bill's owl group are coming along today as well," Jada added. "They have a special licence which allows them to open the nesting boxes. It's against the law for anyone else to do that, unless they have permission."

"They're also experts on the local owl population," Bill said, braking as they approached a roundabout, "so they've been really helpful in rehoming these four owlets."

It didn't take long to reach Ferny Woods. There was a small gravelly car park just off the main road, and when Bill pulled in, Josh saw that there was a blue car already there, with a man and a woman waiting beside it. The man waved when he saw the RSPCA van arrive.

"That's Ian and Mary from our owl group," Bill said, waving back. "They helped us yesterday, too."

Bill let Josh out of the back, then picked up the bird carrier. Josh saw that Ian and Mary had brought a folding ladder and a toolkit with them.

"Hello," he said, feeling a bit shy.

"Nice to meet you," Ian said, shaking his hand. He had tufty white hair and a pair of binoculars slung around his neck.

"Yes, we've heard all about you," said Mary, who had dark hair in a bob and wore a big sparkly necklace. "Your sharp eyes probably saved the lives of four little owls, Josh. Not many people can say that!"

Josh blushed. "I'm glad they're all OK," he said.

"Us too," said Bill, clapping him on the back. "And now I think it's time we found this little fella his brand new home, don't you?"

"Yes," Josh said.

"Then off we go," Bill said. "To the nesting box!"

 **9**

Josh, Bill, Jada, Ian and Mary set off into Ferny Woods, with Bill bringing the bird carrier. Little gave a cheep every now and then, and Josh hoped he wasn't feeling too confused about what was happening. Then, after they'd been walking for about fifteen minutes, they came to a part of the woods Josh recognized. "There it is!" he cried eagerly, pointing up at the nesting box he'd found the week before.

The others came to a halt. "So it is," said Bill, gazing up at the box. "A new home for our last little owl."

Ian propped the ladder against the tree, making sure that the feet were steady, while Jada undid the clasps on the bird carrier. Josh watched, his heart thumping, as Bill climbed up and used a screwdriver to take the lid off the nesting box.

"Will the mother owl be cross at being disturbed?" Josh whispered to Jada. It was the middle of the night for the owls, after all, and he knew his mum didn't like being woken up too early.

She shook her head. "No, the owl group spotted the mother owl leaving the nest earlier, most likely in search of food," she said. "We don't have long, though. The mother only leaves the nest for short periods of time until the chicks are around three weeks old. As for the chicks, they're too young to know what's going on." She slid the box containing the owlet

out of the carrier. "OK, little chap, this is it," she said softly.

"Bye," whispered Josh, with a lump in his throat. He wondered if he'd ever see the owlet again. "I hope you like your new home, Little."

Little stared at Josh for a moment, then blinked his yellow eyes solemnly as if he understood every word. Then Jada passed the box up to Bill, who was still on the ladder.

Josh and the others watched, their heads tipped back, as Bill carefully scooped up the owlet and put him into the nest. They heard a surprised cheep, and then Bill passed the empty box back down to Jada.

Josh blinked. "That was quick," he said.

"The quicker the better, really," Jada said. "That way we don't disturb the other chicks in the nest."

Bill replaced the lid of the nesting box and screwed it back on, then climbed down the ladder looking pleased. "All OK?" asked Mary.

"Absolutely fine," he said. "The other chicks snuggled up to our one immediately."

Josh felt very happy to hear this. He loved thinking of the owlet in a safe, warm nest, with a new mother who'd feed and take care of him from now on. He gazed up at the tree, a tiny bit sad that his part in the owl adventure was now over – but very pleased that the abandoned owlets had all survived, and were now in new homes, thanks to the RSPCA.

"You all right, Josh?" Bill asked, seeing the look on his face.

Josh nodded. "I'm really happy, but also a little sad too," he admitted.

"I know exactly what you mean," said Bill. "I'm sad to say goodbye to that little fella too; I enjoyed looking after him and watching him grow. But what a special feeling it is, knowing that you've helped an animal and given it a new start." He jumped down the last step of the ladder and ruffled Josh's hair. "And at times like this, do you know what we need?" He pulled out the bag of brownies and offered them around. "Here – tuck in," he said. "We've all earned one, I reckon."

"Here's to teamwork, and owl lovers everywhere," Jada said, taking a brownie and biting into it.

"Here's to Josh," said Ian.

"Here's to Little and his new home,"

said Josh, and everyone cheered.

Two weeks later, something very exciting happened: Dad came back from his travels! He was waiting outside school for Josh and Emma on Friday afternoon as a surprise, and picked them both up at once when they ran over to him.

"Daddy!" Emma squealed happily as he swung her around in the air.

"Hi, Dad," Josh said, hugging him for a long, long time. It was only now Dad was back that he realized just how much he'd missed him recently. "I've got so many things to tell you," he began as they walked back to the cottage together.

"I want to know everything!" Dad said, putting an arm around him.

Dad was staying with a friend in the next village but he'd arranged with Mum to bring them home that day. Josh enjoyed telling him all about Little and the other owlets, and how he'd helped the RSPCA and the owl group with Little's rehoming. Once they were back at the cottage, Emma showed Dad her picture of the owls, then did a very dramatic gymnastics display for them all.

"Wow," Dad said at the end. "You two *have* had some adventures while I've been away. Will you take me out to Ferny Woods to show me the nesting box some time, Josh?"

"What, now?" Josh leaped up immediately.

"Why not?" Mum said, smiling. "It's a lovely afternoon. Why don't you change out of your school uniform and go off together while I make tea?"

"Can I go, too?" Emma asked.

"Absolutely," said Dad. "Quick – get changed, both of you! I've got my binoculars and camera all ready."

Two minutes later, Josh, Emma and Dad were heading off to the woods together. Dad was really good at identifying bird calls and picked out the songs of a chiffchaff, a jay and a treecreeper, among others. He took lots of photos of Josh and Emma as they went – and some of

Spotty Dog climbing a tree, too.

"This is it," Josh said, when they reached the nesting box which was now Little's home. "Look, there are lots of new owl pellets under the tree," he added, nudging one with the toe of his welly boot. "The parent owls must have been catching plenty of food for the family."

"That's great," Dad said. "I bet the owlets are much bigger and stronger than when you last saw them, too, Josh. Their feathers will have grown in by now, and the mother will be teaching them how to fly soon."

Josh stared up at the nesting box, wishing and wishing that he could see what was happening inside. How was "his" little owl doing? He hoped he was happy with his new family. *I wonder if I'll ever see him again?* he thought.

A few weeks later, Josh and Tom were in the village shop. It was Friday afternoon again and they both had some money to spend on sweets. Josh was just trying to decide between strawberry fizzbombs and sherbet rockets when he heard an excited gasp from Mrs Miller, the newsagent.

"Here they are! The local heroes!" she cried.

Josh looked round, wondering who Mrs Miller was talking about, but nobody else was there. He turned back to see her smiling broadly at him.

"I mean *you*, Josh — and you as well, Tom," she said. "Haven't you seen this?"

She was holding up a copy of the local newspaper and Josh nearly dropped his sweets when he read the headline. *RESCUED OWLS START NEXT CHAPTER* it said above a large picture of a little owl.

"Whoa!" said Tom, his eyes widening. "Is that one of our owls?"

They hurried over for a closer look at once. "It *is* our owlets," Josh said, reading it quickly. "And it says here that they all survived."

Mrs Miller put the newspaper down on the counter and the two boys pored over the article. " 'Four owl chicks suffered a CRASHING blow back in March when the barn they were nesting in was knocked to the ground in Elderbrook','" Tom read aloud excitedly. " 'Two local boys, Joshua Fraser and Tom Winter. . .' Hey, it's us!"

Josh read on. "'Two local boys, Joshua Fraser and Tom Winter, spotted the abandoned owlets the following day. Weak and hungry, the chicks' lives hung in the balance, but thanks to the boys' quick thinking and the hard work of the local RSPCA team, the owlets were soon on the mend.'"

Tom read the next bit. "'The owlets were rehomed with four feathery foster families, and we are now happy to report that they have all survived and are thriving. According to the local owl group, the owlets are fully fledged and have left their nests.'"

The boys looked at each other, grinning. "They did it," Josh said. "They're out in the wild."

They high-fived each other and Mrs Miller insisted on high-fiving them, too.

"I *do* love a happy ending," she said. "You two had better take a newspaper each – my treat. Go home and show your parents, boys. Won't they be proud of you both?"

Later that night when Josh was getting ready for bed, Emma suddenly charged into his room. "I heard an owl cry!" she exclaimed. "There's an owl outside!"

Josh ran to the window at once and stared out into the dusky garden, Emma

beside him on her tiptoes. The sun had set a while ago, and the sky was becoming dark blue and shadowy.

Then he heard it, too: a high-pitched single cry, rather like a cat's meow. *Keeew!*

"There it is!" he hissed, pointing down the garden to the silver birch tree. It was in silhouette now, like a drawing in a book, but on one of the branches near the top you could definitely see a small, plump bird. *Keeew!* it went again, its head moving as it looked around for prey. "That definitely looks like a little owl."

"Hello, owl," whispered Emma, then turned excitedly to Josh. "Hey, do you think it's Little, and he's flown over from Ferny Woods?"

Josh's heart gave a thump of joy at the thought. "I hope so," he replied, his eyes still glued to the scene. "Hi, Little," he said softly. "It's good to see you again."

As they watched, the little owl turned its head and stretched its wings out suddenly. Then it took off, silently and gracefully, and swooped into the shadows out of view. It was almost as if, Josh thought to himself, the owl had come back to show Josh how grown-up he had become.

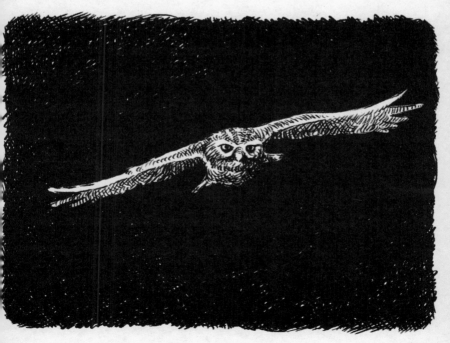

Josh smiled. "Goodnight, Little," he said under his breath.

"Goodbye, Little," Emma echoed, still next to him. "Come and see us again soon." She gazed out into the darkness. "I'm glad we helped him, Josh," she said.

"So am I, Em," Josh replied, feeling very happy. "So am I."

The Real-Life Rescue

Although the characters and birds in Josh's story are fictional, they are based on a real-life rescue in which four baby owls were found orphaned after the building they were nesting in was knocked down.

The baby owls were thought to be just a couple of days old when they were brought to RSPCA Stapeley Grange Wildlife Centre in Cheshire in May, 2011. For the first ten days, they were hand-fed using tweezers, but as the chicks were so young, staff thought their best chances of survival would be fostering them into another nest. This meant an urgent search for barn owl parents who might be able to cope with adding an extra mouth to their existing brood.

With the help of the South Cheshire Barn Owl Group, they found four such breeding pairs with chicks of the same age. Separate families were needed for each owl, as the parents would not have been able to feed more than one extra mouth each. Each rescued chick was carefully slipped into a separate nest and then left to settle into their new families.

David Bromant from the barn owl group said it was the first time they had fostered out so many chicks at once. He said: "We'd never done it on this scale before and were really pleased that it went so well. It was the simplest thing to do. We literally just sneaked the chicks into the nest, and they immediately snuggled up to their new siblings. As long as they are compatible with the age of their existing chicks, barn owl parents will just accept foster chicks as their own. They arrive at the nest with food and just feed to whichever mouths appear."

The group returned to ring all the owls in July, so they could be followed and monitored in the wild, and found that all four chicks had survived. Soon after, they and their siblings left the nests and are now fully fledged back to the wild.

Meet A Real RSPCA Worker

Maxine Bland, Wildlife Supervisor at RSPCA Stapeley Grange

Josh's story is based on a real-life rescue. Could you tell us about a similar rescue you were part of?

In the spring of 2012 a tree was cut down on some farmland. Unfortunately no one checked the tree first and the farmer was genuinely distraught when he discovered it was the nest site of barn owls. An adult barn owl took flight and didn't return. Then a baby chick, only a few days old, was found alive on the ground. The farmer called the RSPCA and an inspector arrived to take the young bird to RSPCA Stapeley Grange Wildlife Centre.

The wildlife centre decided to try to relocate the owlet with wild foster parents, and asked the local owl group to help. Unfortunately no foster family was found and that was when I was called in to help. I set up a box in a safe tree and left mice for him until he was old enough to hunt for himself.

What was the trickiest part of the rescue?

The rescue itself was easy, but in this case it was the rehabilitation that caused a bit of head scratching. Locating a suitable site for the nesting box was tricky, and so was finding enough mice to keep the owl suitably fed. Plus the location of the nesting box, which was up a tree near my home, meant that I had to climb a ladder every evening to drop the mice into the nesting box for the owlet's supper!

Why did you want to work for the RSPCA?

I've always had a strong interest in wildlife in its natural environment. The RSPCA is concerned about animal welfare for all animals, but importantly for me, where its work with wildlife is concerned, they rehabilitate and release back into the wild. We make every effort to minimize contact with the wild animals we care for and this is hugely important to me. It means animals don't become reliant on humans to survive and gives them the best chance of survival when we release them.

What is the best thing about working with wildlife?

It's being part of the journey from beginning to end. Admitting an injured animal or bird, helping it to get well again and seeing it happily released back to the wild — that is the best thing. It's important to understand that nine times out of ten, the injuries we see are caused by man's thoughtlessness — because litter has been dropped, by an act of cruelty, or through a fishing hook or line injury. The team at Stapeley work to put this thoughtlessness right, and when we are successful and release an animal or bird back to the wild it is hugely satisfying. Seeing them fly off or scamper into the woodland free again to enjoy their life is definitely the best part!

To find out more about the work
the RSPCA do, go to:
www.rspca.org.uk

A Wildlife Assistant holding a young little owl

Four little owls perching

Facts About Owls

- There are about 220 different species of owls.

- Baby owls are called "owlets".

- Owls hunt insects, small mammals and other birds.

- Like all birds, owls do not have teeth and so they have to swallow their food whole.

- They regurgitate pellets of food they can't digest, such as bone, fur and feathers.

- Owls have powerful claws called "talons" which help them hunt their prey.

- They are farsighted, which means they can't see things close by very clearly.

Based on a real-life animal rescue

RSPCA

The Abandoned Kitten

Buying this book helps the RSPCA save animals' lives

Take a sneak peek at an extract from another exciting story based on a real-life animal rescue!

With Mum out, and the boys supposedly tidying their messy bedroom, Lily decided to get on with her homework. She had some maths puzzles to work out and a list of spellings to learn for a test. It was hard to concentrate, though, when she kept thinking about the animals Mum might be looking after at the RSPCA centre. She hoped everything was OK.

"Have you heard from Mum yet?" she asked Dad when he came into the kitchen a bit later.

Dad shook his head. "Not a sausage,"

he said. "How's the homework going? Do you need any help?"

Lily closed her exercise book. "I'll do it later," she said, wrinkling her nose.

Dad gave her a thoughtful look, as if he knew her mind was elsewhere. "Tell you what," he said, "why don't we make a nice cake for tea? Mum deserves a treat for working so hard."

Lily smiled. "Good idea," she said.

Once they'd washed their hands, Lily helped weigh out the butter and sugar, and tipped them into a big mixing bowl. "It won't be long until I need to make a special cake for you," Dad said, getting eggs out of the fridge, "what with your birthday next month. Have you thought about what kind of cake you might like this year?"

"Chocolate, please," Lily said at once. Dad was a really good baker, and made the most amazing cakes for everyone. Last year, he'd baked her a cake in the shape of a dog's head, complete with a pink iced tongue hanging out of its smiling mouth. "But that's still ages away."

"Ahh, you wait, the weeks will fly by," Dad said, passing Lily a wooden spoon. "Right – let's get mixing."

Lily enjoyed helping Dad in the kitchen. He was an artist, illustrating storybooks and greetings cards for a living, and he saw cookery as another chance to be creative. Some of his cake decorations turned out almost as beautiful as his paintings and drawings!

Lily's favourite picture by Dad was one that hung above the mantelpiece in the living room. In the painting, the Harts were riding on the back of a smiling green dragon, looking as if they were flying off to have a wonderful adventure

together. Even Meg was included in the painting, sitting on the dragon's back with Lily's arms around her. It made Lily smile every time she looked at it.

"Hmm," Dad said as Lily sifted the flour into the bowl. "What can we put in this cake to give it some extra zing?"

"Lemon juice?" Lily suggested.

"Good thinking," he replied. "And how about a handful of chocolate chips and some grated orange zest, too?"

"Yum," Lily said approvingly. "Mum's going to love it."

The cake smelled delicious as it baked, and Lily helped Dad with the washing up. She began to feel hungry and glanced up at the clock to see when it would be teatime. To her surprise, it was almost five o'clock already. Mum had been gone for hours now! She and the rest of the

RSPCA team must be really busy. When was she going to come home?

Once the cake had cooled, Lily and Dad covered it in white glossy icing, then decorated it with candied orange and lemon slices around the edge. Then Dad's phone buzzed.

"Aha!" he said, reading a text. "That's your mum. She'll be home in about fifteen minutes." He peered in the fridge. "How does pizza for tea sound?"

Lily grinned. "Sounds perfect."

A short while later, Meg barked and they heard the key turn in the front door. "Mum's home!" Max cried.

"Brilliant timing," Dad said, switching off the oven and putting a handful of cutlery on the table.

"We're in the kitchen!" Lily called.

Mum appeared holding an animal carrier. "Hi, everyone," she said, setting it carefully on the table. Then she sniffed. "Mmm, something smells nice in here."

"Hi, Mum," Lily said. "Is everything all right? What's in there?"

Dad went over to kiss Mum and looked into the cat carrier. His eyes widened as he saw what she'd brought in. "Oh my goodness," he said. "What have we here?"

"Three little babies who need some extra looking after," Mum replied, then smiled at Lily and the boys. "Come over and have a peep – but be really quiet, won't you? I don't want them to be scared."

Lily was bursting with curiosity as she, Jacob and Max went over to see. Mum carefully opened the carrier and Lily

gasped with excitement as she saw three
bundles of fluff inside, curled up on a
soft blue blanket, with a hot-water bottle
keeping them warm. They were the
tiniest kittens she'd ever seen!

"Oh, Mum," she whispered, resisting
the urge to reach in and stroke them. She
knew that they might be very poorly, and
that she needed to check before touching
them. "They're so small. Are they OK?"

Mum gave her a smile. "I'm going to do my best to look after them," she said, which didn't really answer Lily's question.

"What *are* they?" Max asked, peering in. "Are they hamsters?"

"They're kittens!" Lily replied.

"We think they're only a week old," Mum added, "which is why their eyes haven't opened yet. They're pretty helpless right now."

"They don't look like proper kittens," Jacob said, hanging back doubtfully.

Mum smiled. "They're just babies," she said. "And they don't have a mummy to look after them, so I'm going to have to be their mummy for a short while, and take care of them here. Just like a real cat mummy, I'll be taking them everywhere with me. So when I'm at home they'll be here, and when I go to work they'll come with me as well!"

Meg seemed curious about the new arrivals. She kept walking back and forth, and sniffing the air around the table. Then she made a funny whining sound.

"Good girl. It's all right," Mum told her, reaching down and stroking her silky head. "You're still top dog in this house, don't worry."

Lily gazed in at the kittens. One was black all over, another was black with white paws and a white mark on its face, and the third and smallest kitten was a tabby, with grey and black markings. They were very sweet with their crumpled-looking ears and tightly shut eyes, but Jacob was right: they didn't look like other kittens she'd seen. She'd always thought of kittens as being full of energy, tumbling over each other

and playing with everything in sight. These three, by contrast, seemed hardly able to move. No wonder Mum had called them "poor little things" on the phone!

Just then, the black kitten opened its mouth and gave a teeny-tiny mew, and Lily's heart melted at the sound.

"I think somebody's hungry again," Mum said. "Let's give kitty a feed."

"Can I help?" Lily asked.

"Of course," Mum said. "Without their mummy around, we need to feed them with special kitten milk. I've brought some home with me."

"What happened to their mum?" Lily asked, watching as Mum popped the lid off a large tin full of creamy-white powder. "Is she still at the centre?"

Mum shook her head. "We don't know where she is, unfortunately," she replied, tipping a scoop of powder into a jug and measuring out boiled water from the kettle. "All we know is that these three were found at the end of a garden in the next village – soaking wet and shivering. The mother cat was nowhere to be seen."

"Poor babies," Lily said, feeling sad. She hated to think of them lying there, cold and wet, without their mum to take care of them.

"The lady who brought them into the centre said it was only by chance that she found them at all," Mum went on. "She was just nipping out to the shop when she spotted them under the hedge in her front garden. She got them to us in the nick of time."

Jacob looked upset. "Why did their mummy leave them there?" he asked.

"Maybe she didn't have a choice," Mum replied, whisking the powder into the water until it looked like smooth, creamy milk. "There," she said. "This substitute milk has all the goodness they need to help them grow properly but isn't too rich for their little tummies. Kittens don't drink the milk we drink."

More squeaks were coming from the cat carrier now, and Lily peered in to see all three kittens mewing pitifully.

"Nearly ready, guys," she said softly.
"Milk's on its way."

"Why don't you wash your hands and stroke them very gently?" Mum suggested to Lily, filling a dropper with the milk. "That might comfort them until I can feed them all."

Lily quickly washed her hands and stroked the tiny kittens with her finger. Their bodies were soft and warm. "It's all right," she whispered. "Don't worry. We know you're hungry."

"I'm hungry, too," Max said at that moment, suddenly remembering the pizzas. "Are *we* allowed something to eat?"

"Definitely," said Dad. "Wash your hands and then sit at the table, boys. Pizza number one is about to be served and pizza number two can wait until the kitten feeding is over."

"I can wait till later," Lily said at once. "Shall I carry on helping you, Mum?"

"Yes, please," Mum replied. "If you could keep comforting the other two while I feed the first one, that would be wonderful."

Everyone watched Mum as she scooped the black-and-white kitten out of the cat carrier. It was so small it easily fitted into her hand – just a handful of fluff with a tiny scrap of a tail. Lily glanced up at the window and saw that the rain was still pouring down outside. She was so glad the kittens had been found.

Meg came over to smell the kitten, but Dad gently pulled her away by her collar. "Let's look from a distance, Meg," he said, patting her side. "Good girl."

Mum sat down with the kitten cuddled on her lap and then, using a small dropper, she carefully squeezed a few drops of warm milk into the kitten's open pink mouth.

The kitten spluttered a little before swallowing the milk. Then it opened its mouth again for more.

Lily watched, still gently stroking the other two. "Is that one a boy or a girl kitten, Mum?" she asked.

"This is one of the boys," Mum replied. "There are two boys and a girl."

"Two boys and a girl, eh?" Dad said, putting plates of pizza slices on the table for Jacob and Max. "Now where have I heard that before?"

"The brothers are the coolest," Max said immediately, nudging Jacob.

Jacob nodded, his mouth full. "The brothers are the best," he agreed.

Lily caught Mum's eye and they both smiled. "Which is the girl?" Lily asked.

"The little tabby," Mum said. "She's the smallest of the bunch, which probably means she's the youngest."

Lily stroked the tabby, who had pretty stripy markings. "You're definitely the cutest," she whispered to her. "Don't listen to my brothers, OK?"

"There," said Mum after a few minutes, when the black-and-white kitten had drunk enough. "One down, two to feed."

"That was quick," Dad commented, forking some salad into his mouth.

"Their tummies are so small it doesn't take long to fill them up," Mum replied. "Although it does mean that they'll be hungry again in a few hours." She gently returned the black-and-white kitten to the blanket and took out the all-black kitten, who was squeaking sorrowfully. "Your turn now, little one," she said soothingly.

"So the kittens will need feeding again when we're in bed?" Lily asked. "And in the middle of the night?"

"Yes," said Mum. "Every two and a half

hours or thereabouts. Just like you three when you were tiny babies."

"Cool," said Max. "Can we stay up all night, too?"

"No chance." Dad said, laughing. "Finish that pizza, then you can have some cake."

Lily had been so excited by the kittens, she'd forgotten all about the cake. "Oh yes!" she said. "Me and Dad baked it especially for you, Mum."

"Wow," Mum said, looking pleased. "Kind children, a pizza-baking husband and a cake . . . what a lucky mum I am."

Woof! went Meg. "Not forgetting the best dog ever," Mum said, with a smile.

Collect the whole series...

Based on a real-life animal rescue
Little Lost Hedgehog
Buying this book helps the RSPCA save animals' lives

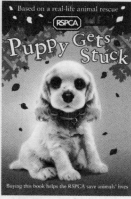
Based on a real-life animal rescue
Puppy Gets Stuck
Buying this book helps the RSPCA save animals' lives

Based on a real-life animal rescue
Lamb All Alone
Buying this book helps the RSPCA save animals' lives

Based on a real-life animal rescue
The Abandoned Kitten
Buying this book helps the RSPCA save animals' lives

Based on a real-life animal rescue
Little Owl Needs a Home
Buying this book helps the RSPCA save animals' lives

Based on a real-life animal rescue
Bunny Needs a Friend
Buying this book helps the RSPCA save animals' lives

Coming in
March 2014

Join the RSPCA!

You'll receive:

- **six issues of** *animal action* **magazine**
- **a brilliant welcome pack**
- **a FAB joining gift**
- **and a FREE gift with every issue.**

Go to: **www.rspca.org.uk/ theclub**

Ask an adult to call: **0300 123 0346** and pay by debit/credit card.

ALL FOR £15! (£22 OVERSEAS)